The Giant Leaf

DAVY LIU

For His Glory

Grateful acknowledgement
to Douglas Wood and Laura Derico
for their creative input and insight.

The Giant Leaf
ISBN: 9781937212278
Updated Edition - First Printing: July 2016
Published by Green Egg Media, Inc.
Irvine, California
greeneggmediagroup.com

Printed in Korea through Codra Enterprises, Inc.
codra.com

The dream was always the same. Kendu floated in an
endless blue, beneath a giant leaf. And he was free.

But Kendu was not free.

Each sun-drenched day, Kendu and the other foxes were forced to dig holes to hold the eggs of the Great Beasts.

They must dig and dig and never stop digging, even for a moment. If they did not dig the holes, the Great Beasts would not protect them.

Without their protection, the foxes might be eaten by the forever-hungry monster that lived Out There.

One day Kendu said to himself, "We are being protected just so we can work as slaves! What good is that?!"

After that, Kendu thought of running away every day.

One afternoon, the Great Beasts ate until their bellies were almost bursting. They all fell into a deep, deep sleep.

Kendu knew this was his chance. In a flash, he ran away as fast and as far as he could go.

Kendu ran until day became night.

When he stopped to rest, he suddenly felt alone and afraid. He didn't know where to go! He looked up just in time to see the moonlight breaking through the clouds.

What was that? Kendu saw a gazelle standing on a mountain peak. As the animal turned its head, its long, slender antlers formed a shape. It was a shape Kendu knew very well.

Kendu knew what he must do. Find the giant leaf!

Kendu was eager to hunt for the leaf. But he was sooo tired!
The sleepy fox lay down in the soft grass. Soon he was
dreaming of the giant leaf again.

As the sun's first rays warmed the earth, Kendu awoke with a smile.

"Leaves are on branches," he thought. "And branches are on trees!"

Kendu headed straight for the forest to look for giant trees with giant leaves.

The thick branches overhead blocked out the sunlight. Kendu decided he needed to climb a tall tree to get a better view.

"You're wasting your time, bushy tail!" A monkey stared down at Kendu. "I've searched all day long! This is the only golden-sweet I can find."

"I don't want golden-sweets. I want to find giant trees!" Kendu replied.

"Good luck! Those are gone too! Someone has been chopping down all the best trees!"

Kendu slipped off the branch with a thump.

"Sorry my friend! I'm Yitzak. I have not seen you before. Why are you looking for giant trees?"

"My name is Kendu. And I'm looking for a giant leaf that I have seen in my dreams!"

"Ohhh! I have seen this leaf in my dreams too!" Yitzak said. "Every night! It holds mountains of golden-sweets...nice and mushy and YUMMY!"

"So where can we find it?" Kendu asked.

Yitzak scratched his head. "Hmmm. I guess it could be in the Wilds, the deepest part of the forest."

But as he spoke, Yitzak's eyes grew big as he looked all around. It was as if he thought someone else might be listening.

Then he whispered, "But you don't want to go there! That's where the Animal Eater lives! They say his ribcage is the size of a mountain!"

"I'm not afraid! I must find that leaf!" Kendu said. He started walking deeper into the forest.

"Come with me, Yitzak! Let's go find that mountain of golden-sweets!" Kendu yelled back to his new friend.

"Uh . . . sure!" Yitzak said. But his heart was pounding inside his chest.

Two nights came and went as the two friends walked in the great forest.

Yitzak never stopped talking. And Kendu never stopped searching for the giant leaf.

On the third day, a koala jumped down from a tree and landed right in front of Kendu and Yitzak.

"Please help me!" she cried. "My Gula is gone! I think the Animal Eater took him!"

Delia, the koala, told them how her mate had gone searching for food. He never returned.

"Every day more animals go missing!" Delia was very upset. "And every day more tree stumps appear!"

"But every night I have a wonderful dream. Gula and I are in the Wilds together. We are very happy as we ride on a giant leaf."

Kendu couldn't believe it! "You dream of the giant leaf too? Then you must come with us! Somehow we must stop that Animal Eater."

"Or maybe, we will find Gula, and he can stop the Animal Eater?" Yitzak said. His face was full of fear.

"Don't worry, Yitzak! The two of us can handle anything," Kendu said.

"You mean the three of us!" Delia smiled.

It wasn't long before they reached the dark, deep part of the forest, known as the Wilds. Just as the three new friends stepped into the shadows, a bright light shot through the sky! The clouds rumbled!

There before them was a sight they would remember forever. It was the Animal Eater!

"Look! There are animals inside its mouth!" Yitzak yelled.

"Shhh!" Kendu stared into the darkness. "Wait! Those animals are alive!"

Delia squinted. "Can you see my Gula?"

Another flash of light came. In that instant, Kendu and his friends saw the long, slender antlers of the gazelle. It was standing right in the mouth of the Animal Eater!

With the next flash, the gazelle was gone.

Big, fat raindrops started falling from the sky.
"Let's go!" Kendu shouted. The rain plopped heavily onto the ground.

Yitzak and Delia were afraid. But they followed Kendu as he ran toward the mouth of the Animal Eater.

But they were still a long way away. And the water did not stop coming.

Soon a stream rose up and wound its way through the forest. The stream rushed through the trees, pushing away bushes and logs. Then it swept away Kendu!

Yitzak acted fast. Grabbing Delia, the monkey leaped onto a giant lily pad in the water. When Kendu came within reach, Yitzak swooped the fox up in his long arms.

The waters rose. Puddles became streams. Streams became rivers. And rivers turned into oceans.

Days blended into nights as the dark clouds hid the light. Kendu began to lose hope. We'll never make it to the Animal Eater now, he thought.

Suddenly a strong wind swirled the waters around them and lifted the three friends high up on a mountain of waves.

"Hold on tight to the lily pads!" Yitzak cried.

The wind pulled them up, up, up into the air!

Then the three were floating down, down, down, like butterflies.

The wind carried them gently down until they landed safely—at the mouth of the Animal Eater!

Peeking in, they saw animals of every kind.

In no time, Yitzak found a mountain of golden-sweets. All his fears and worries were gone. Now he could fill his empty stomach!

"I'm going to be happy here!" Yitzak stuffed his mouth with food.

A sweet monkey named Windy laughed at silly Yitzak. He swallowed and shared his fruit with her.

"Very happy!" he said. Windy smiled.

Delia climbed up a branch and bumped right into her Gula!

He told her how he had gotten lost in the woods. He dreamed of Delia sitting on a giant leaf in the Wilds. When he woke up, he went searching for her there.

"When the waters began, I was afraid I had lost you forever," said Gula. "I'm so thankful we are both safe inside the Animal Eater."

"Me too." Delia hugged Gula tight.

Kendu was happy to see his friends safe and warm. But one thing troubled him.

Where was the giant leaf?

He searched through the stables. No giant leaf. Instead, he found a surprise. There above a warm den was his own name, carved in wood!

"Hello," said a friendly fox with a kind face. "I'm Reia." She nodded up at her name on the other sign. "I guess someone knew we would come."

She smiled at him, and Kendu felt as if he had come home.

In the days to come, Kendu told Reia the stories of the Great Beasts and his life as a slave. He told her of his dreams of the giant leaf. And she told him of her dreams too, that had led her to the Animal Eater.

Then one day they heard the voice of the two-feeter who lived with them. He often brought food for all the animals. But this time, he shouted, "Land, my friends! Land! We are home!"

"Come on! Let's go!" Reia said, and ran. Kendu chased her, and together they leaped off the edge of the Animal Eater.

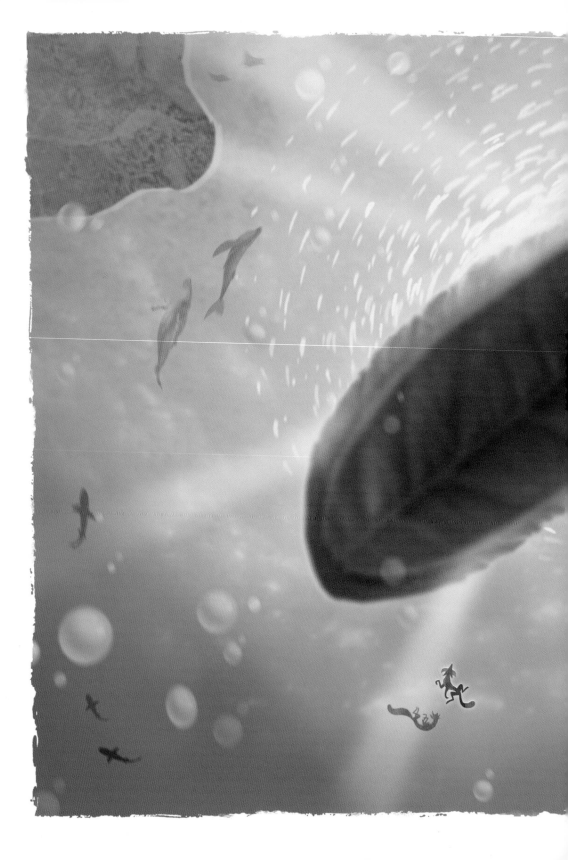

Kendu had found the giant leaf at last.
And just like in his dreams, he was free.

The story of the giant leaf spread among all the
animals in all the lands. . . . And it spreads still today.

Artist and Author Davy Liu immigrated to the United States at age 13. Within a few months, his talent for drawing and painting was discovered.

At age 19 Davy began a career in feature films working for Disney Studios, Warner Bros and Industrial Light and Magic. His work has appeared in *The Beauty and The Beast*, *Aladdin*, *Mulan*, *The Lion King* and *Star Wars Episode I*.

Every year Davy speaks to over 250,000 people, sharing his inspirational story of overcoming the incredible odds he faced in his youth.

To learn how to draw characters from the Invisible Tails series and to see Davy's speaking schedule, go to InvisibleTails.com